Cock-a-Doodle Quack! Quack!

Ivor Baddiel and Sophie Jubb
Illustrated by Ailie Busby

PICTURE CORGI

For Hamish,
who always knows what to say
AB

For Ruby and Art, who always know
how to wake us up
IB & SJ

COCK A DOODLE QUACK! QUACK!
A PICTURE CORGI BOOK 978 0 552 54888 5 (from January 2007)
0 552 54888 X

First published in Great Britain by Picture Corgi,
an imprint of Random House Children's Books

This edition published 2006

3 5 7 9 10 8 6 4 2

Text copyright © Ivor Baddiel and Sophie Jubb, 2006
Illustrations copyright © Ailie Busby, 2006

The right of Ivor Baddiel, Sophie Jubb and Ailie Busby to be identified
as the authors and illustrator of this work has been asserted in accordance
with the Copyright, Designs and Patents Act 1988.

Picture Corgi Books are published by Random House Children's Books,
61–63 Uxbridge Road, London W5 5SA,
a division of The Random House Group Ltd,
in Australia by Random House Australia (Pty) Ltd,
20 Alfred Street, Milsons Point, Sydney, NSW 2061, Australia,
in New Zealand by Random House New Zealand Ltd,
18 Poland Road, Glenfield, Auckland 10, New Zealand,
and in South Africa by Random House (Pty) Ltd,
Isle of Houghton, Corner Boundary Road & Carse O'Gowrie,
Houghton 2198, South Africa

THE RANDOM HOUSE GROUP Limited Reg. No. 954009
www.**kids**at**random**house.co.uk

A CIP catalogue record for this book is available from the British Library.

Printed and bound in China

Once upon a time there was a baby cockerel.

It was his job to wake everybody up in the morning, but he didn't know how. He didn't know what to say.

So, he went to see the pigs.
"Hello, pigs. It's my job to wake everyone
up in the morning, but I don't know
what to say. What do YOU say?"

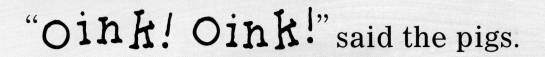

"**Oink! Oink!**" said the pigs.

"That's good," said Baby Cockerel.
"I'll try that tomorrow."

The next morning as the sun was rising,
the baby cockerel took a deep breath
and at the top of his voice he said,

OODLE~OINK~OINK!

But nothing happened.

NOBODY WOKE UP.

So, the baby cockerel
went to see the cows.

"Hello, cows," he said. "It's my job to wake everyone up in the morning, but I don't know what to say. What do YOU say?"

"Moo! Moo!" said the cows.

"Ooh yes.
That's good,"
said Baby Cockerel.
"I'll try that tomorrow."

The next morning as the sun was rising,
the baby cockerel took a really deep breath
and at the top of his voice he said,

COCK~A~D

OODLE~MOO~MOO!

But nothing happened.

NOBODY WOKE UP.

So, he went to see the ducks.
He said, "Hello, ducky ducks. It's my job
to wake everyone up in the morning, but
I don't know what to say. What do YOU say?"

"Quack! Quack!" said the ducks.
"Oh, that's really good," said Baby Cockerel.
"I'll try that tomorrow."

The next morning just as the sun was rising,
the baby cockerel took a very deep breath
and said,

COCK~A~DOOD

But nothing happened.

NOBODY WOKE UP.

The baby cockerel was very sad.
"What's the matter?" asked Cat.
Baby Cockerel said nothing.

"Oh dear," said the cat. "I can tell something's wrong. You'd better go and see the wise old owl. He'll know what to do."

So, Baby Cockerel walked up
to the huge barn where Owl lived.
He knocked on the door.
"Come in," said Owl.

"Please can you help me?" said Baby Cockerel.
"It's my job to wake everyone up in the
morning but I don't know what to say."
The wise old owl smiled.
"My friend, tomorrow, as the sun is rising,
go down to the farm gate and sit there quietly.

Don't say anything.
Just listen. Then you
will know exactly
what to do."

That night
Baby Cockerel
hardly slept at all.
He was very puzzled.

He still
didn't know
how he was going
to wake everyone up.

At last, the sun began to rise.
The baby cockerel got up and
walked down the lane.
He stood on the farm
gate and *listened*
carefully.

It was very quiet. Baby Cockerel
couldn't hear anything at all.
But he remembered the
wise old owl's words
and he *listened*
again.

Then, the baby cockerel heard a noise
coming from the farm next door.
He *listened* very, very carefully.
He tried to copy the noise.

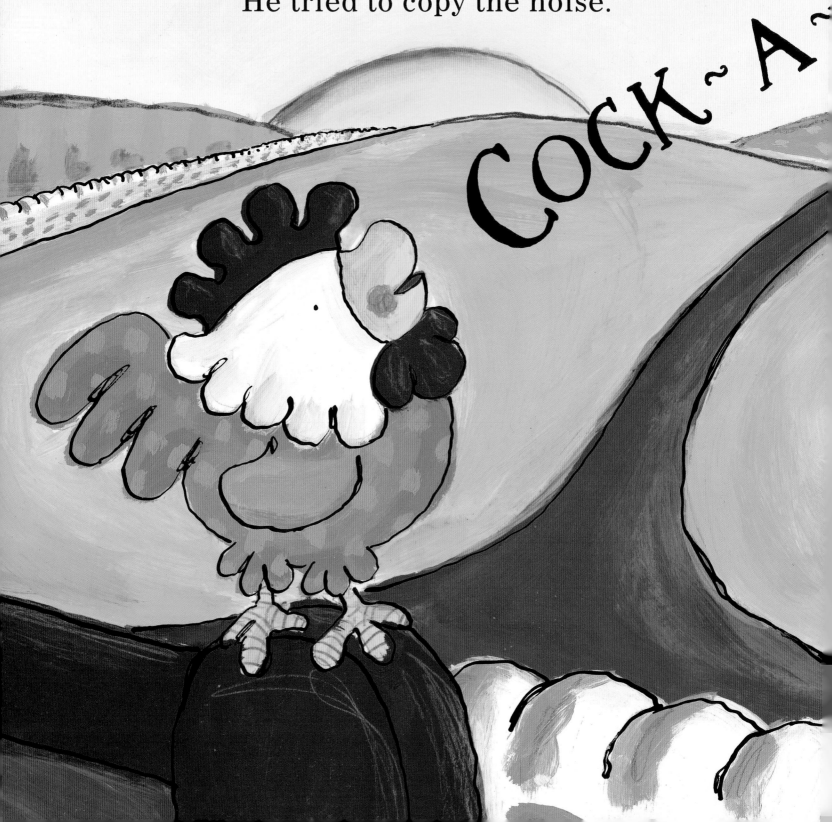

COCK~A~

NOODLE~NOO!

NOTHING HAPPENED.

No one woke up.
He *listened* again,
even more carefully.

He took a deep breath.

COCK

A~POODLE~POO!

STILL NOBODY WOKE UP.

He *listened* as carefully
and as quietly as he could.

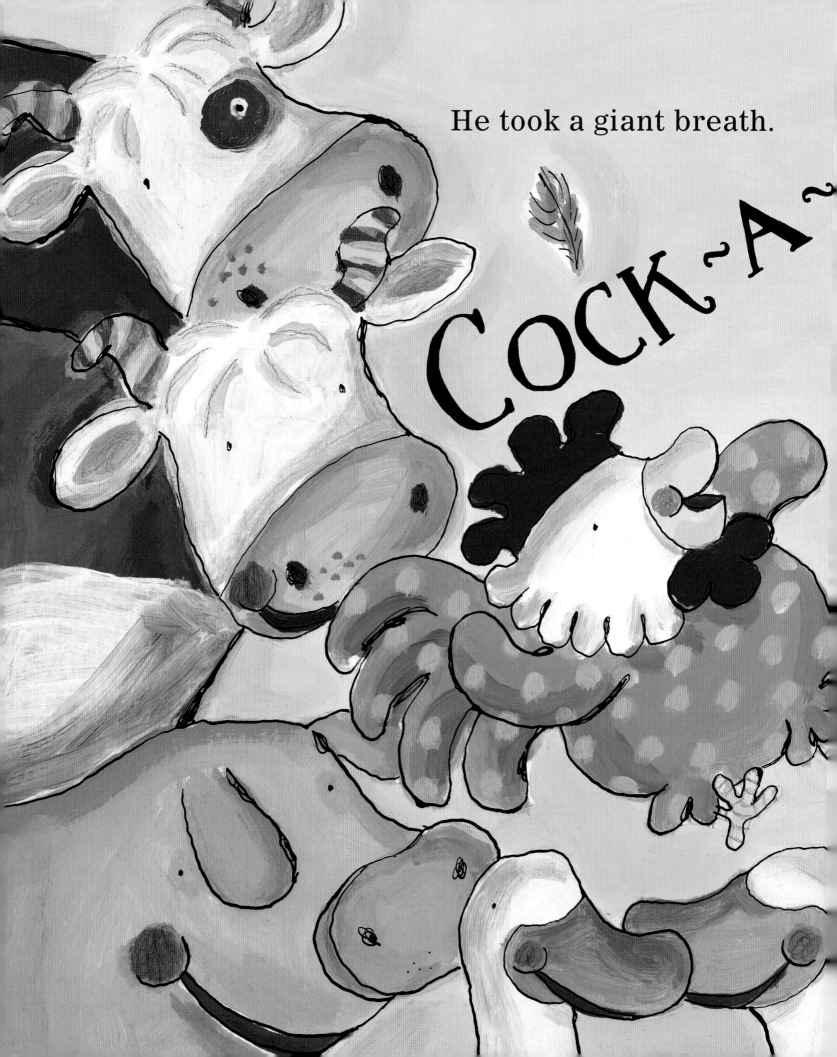

He took a giant breath.

COCK~A~

At last Baby Cockerel knew how to
wake everybody up.

COCK~A~DOODLE~DOO!

He was so pleased and happy and so tired
that he fell fast asleep.

But he was up early again the next morning . . .